A. A. MILNE

Pooh Goes Visiting and Pooh and Piglet Nearly Catch a Woozle

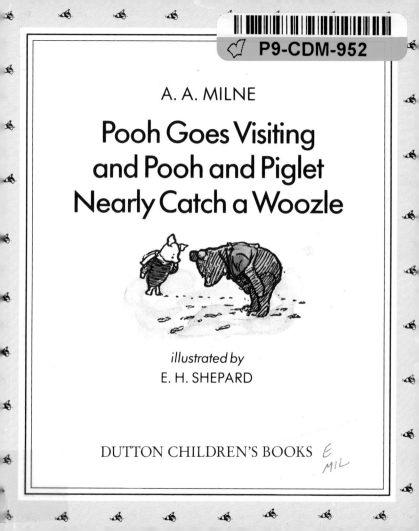

illustrated by
E. H. SHEPARD

DUTTON CHILDREN'S BOOKS

front of the glass: *Tra-la-la, tra-la-la*, as he stretched up as high as he could go, and then *Tra-la-la, tra-la – oh, help! – la*, as he tried to

reach his toes. After breakfast he had said it over and over to himself until he had learnt it off by heart, and now he was humming it right through, properly. It went like this:

Tra-la-la, tra-la-la,
Tra-la-la, tra-la-la,
Rum-tum-tiddle-um-um.
Tiddle-iddle, tiddle-iddle,
Tiddle-iddle, tiddle-iddle,
Rum-tum-tum-tiddle-um.

Well, he was humming this hum to himself, and walking gaily along, wondering what

Pooh Goes Visiting and Pooh and Piglet Nearly Catch a Woozle

Edward Bear, known to his friends as Winnie-the-Pooh, or Pooh for short, was walking through the Forest one day, humming proudly to himself. He had made up a little hum that very morning, as he was doing his Stoutness Exercises in

everybody else was doing, and what it felt like, being somebody else, when suddenly he came to a sandy bank, and in the bank was a large hole.

'Aha!' said Pooh. *(Rum-tum-tiddle-um-tum.)* 'If I know anything about anything, that hole means Rabbit,' he said, 'and Rabbit means Company,' he said, 'and Company means Food and Listening-to-Me-Humming and such like.

'Rum-tum-tum-tiddle-um.'

So he bent down, put his head into the hole, and called out: 'Is anybody at home?'

There was a sudden scuffling noise from inside the hole, and then silence.

'What I said was, "Is anybody at home?"' called out Pooh very loudly.

'No!' said a voice; and then added. 'You needn't shout so loud. I heard you quite well the first time.'

'Bother!' said Pooh. 'Isn't there anybody here at all?'

'Nobody.'

Winnie-the-Pooh took his head out of

the hole, and thought for a little, and he thought to himself, 'There must be somebody there, because somebody must have *said* "Nobody."' So he put his head back in the hole, and said: 'Hallo, Rabbit, isn't that you?'

'No,' said Rabbit, in a different sort of voice this time.

'But isn't that Rabbit's voice?'

'I don't *think* so,' said Rabbit. 'It isn't *meant* to be.'

'Oh!' said Pooh. He took his head out of the hole, and had another think, and then he put it back, and said: 'Well, could you very kindly tell me where Rabbit is?'

'He has gone to see his friend Pooh Bear, who is a great friend of his.'

'But this *is* Me!' said Bear, very much surprised.

'What sort of Me?'

'Pooh Bear.'

'Are you sure?' said Rabbit, still more surprised.

'Quite, quite sure,' said Pooh.
'Oh, well, then, come in.'
So Pooh pushed and pushed and pushed his

way through the hole, and at last he got in.

'You were quite right,' said Rabbit, looking at him all over. 'It *is* you. Glad to see you.'

'Who did you think it was?'

'Well, I wasn't sure. You know how it is in the Forest. One can't have *anybody* coming into one's house. One has to be *careful*. What about a mouthful of something?'

Pooh always liked a little something at eleven o'clock in the morning, and he was very glad to see Rabbit getting out the plates and mugs; and when Rabbit said, 'Honey or condensed milk with your bread?' he was so excited that he said, 'Both,' and then, so as not to seem greedy, he added, 'But don't bother about the bread, please.' And for a long time after that he said nothing . . . until at last, humming to himself in a rather sticky voice, he got up, shook Rabbit lovingly by the paw, and said that he must be going on.

'Must you?' said Rabbit politely.

'Well,' said Pooh, 'I could stay a little longer if it – if you—' and he tried very hard to look in the direction of the larder.

'As a matter of fact,' said Rabbit, 'I was going out myself directly.'

'Oh well, then, I'll be going on. Good-bye.'

'Well, good-bye, if you're sure you won't have any more.'

'*Is* there any more?' asked Pooh quickly.

Rabbit took the covers off the dishes, and said, 'No, there wasn't.'

'I thought not,' said Pooh, nodding to himself. 'Well, good-bye, I must be going on.'

So he started to climb out of the hole. He pulled with his front paws, and pushed with his back paws, and in a little while his nose was out in the open again . . . and then his ears . . . and then his front paws . . . and then his shoulders . . . and then—

'Oh, bother!' said Pooh. I shall have to go on.'

'Oh, help!' said Pooh. 'I'd better go back.'

'I can't do either!' said Pooh. 'Oh, help *and* bother!'

Now, by this time Rabbit wanted to go for a walk too, and finding the front door full, he went out by the back door, and came round to Pooh, and looked at him.

'Hallo, are you stuck?' he asked.

'N-no,' said Pooh carelessly. 'Just resting and thinking and humming to myself.'

'Here, give us a paw.'

Pooh Bear stretched out a paw, and Rabbit pulled and pulled and pulled. . . .

'*Ow!*' cried Pooh. 'You're hurting!'

'The fact is,' said Rabbit, 'you're stuck.'

'It all comes,' said Pooh crossly, 'of not having front doors big enough.'

'It all comes,' said Rabbit sternly, 'of eating too much. I thought at the time,' said Rabbit, 'only I didn't like to say anything,' said Rabbit, 'that one of us was eating too much,' said Rabbit, 'and I knew it wasn't *me*,' he said. 'Well, well, I shall go and fetch Christopher Robin.'

Christopher Robin lived at the other end of the Forest, and when he came back with

Rabbit, and saw the front half of Pooh, he said, 'Silly old Bear,' in such a loving voice that everybody felt quite hopeful again.

'I was just beginning to think,' said Bear, sniffing slightly, 'that Rabbit might never be able to use his front door again. And I should *hate* that,' he said.

'So should I,' said Rabbit.

'Use his front door again?' said Christopher Robin. 'Of course he'll use his front door again.'

'Good,' said Rabbit.

'If we can't pull you out, Pooh, we might push you back.'

Rabbit scratched his whiskers thoughtfully, and pointed out that, when once Pooh was pushed back, he was back, and of course nobody was more glad to see Pooh than *he* was, still there it was, some lived in trees and some lived underground, and—

'You mean I'd *never* get out?' said Pooh.

'I mean,' said Rabbit, 'that having got *so*

far, it seems a pity to waste it.'

Christopher Robin nodded.

'Then there's only one thing to be done,' he said. 'We shall have to wait for you to get thin again.'

'How long does getting thin take?' asked Pooh anxiously.

'About a week, I should think.'

'But I can't stay here for a *week*!'

'You can *stay* here all right, silly old Bear. It's getting you out which is so difficult.'

'We'll read to you,' said Rabbit cheerfully.

'And I hope it won't snow,' he added. 'And I say, old fellow, you're taking up a good deal of room in my house – *do* you mind if I use your back legs as a towel-horse? Because, I mean, there they are – doing nothing – and it would be very convenient just to hang the towels on them.'

'A week!' said Pooh gloomily. '*What about meals?*'

'I'm afraid no meals,' said Christopher Robin,

'because of getting thin quicker. But we *will* read to you.'

Bear began to sigh, and then found he couldn't because he was so tightly stuck; and a tear rolled down his eye, as he said:

'Then would you read a Sustaining Book, such as would help and comfort a Wedged Bear in Great Tightness?'

So for a week Christopher Robin read that sort of book at the North end of Pooh, and

Rabbit hung his washing on the South end . . .

and in between Bear felt himself getting
slenderer and slenderer. And at the end of the
week Christopher Robin said,

'Now!'

So he took hold of Pooh's front paws and
Rabbit took hold of Christopher Robin, and all
Rabbit's friends and relations took hold of
Rabbit, and they all pulled together. . . .

And for a long time Pooh only said '*Ow!*' ...

And '*Oh!*' ...

And then, all of a sudden, he said '*Pop!*' just as if a cork were coming out of a bottle.

And Christopher Robin and Rabbit and all Rabbit's friends and relations went head-over-heels backwards ...

and on the top of them came
Winnie-the-Pooh – free!
    So, with a nod of thanks
to his friends,
he went on with his walk
through the forest,
humming proudly to himself.
But Christopher Robin
looked after him lovingly,
and said to himself,
'Silly old Bear!'

The Piglet lived in a very grand house in the middle of a beech-tree, and the beech-tree was in the middle of the Forest, and the Piglet

lived in the middle of the house. Next to his house was a piece of broken board which had: 'TRESPASSERS W' on it. When Christopher Robin asked the Piglet what it meant, he said it was his grandfather's name, and had been in the family for a long time. Christopher Robin said you *couldn't* be called Trespassers W, and Piglet said yes, you could, because his grandfather was, and it was short for Trespassers Will, which was short for Trespassers William.

And his grandfather had had two names in case he lost one – Trespassers after an uncle, and William after Trespassers.

'I've got two names,' said Christopher Robin carelessly.

'Well, there you are, that proves it,' said Piglet.

One fine winter's day when Piglet was brushing away the snow in front of his house, he happened to look up, and there was Winnie-the-Pooh. Pooh was walking round and round in a circle, thinking of something else, and when Piglet called to him, he just went on walking.

'Hallo!' said Piglet, 'what are *you* doing?'

'Hunting,' said Pooh.

'Hunting what?'

'Tracking something,' said Winnie-the-Pooh very mysteriously.

'Tracking what?' said Piglet, coming closer.

'That's just what I ask myself. I ask myself, What?'

'What do you think you'll answer?'

'I shall have to wait until I catch up with it,'

said Winnie-the-Pooh. 'Now, look there.' He pointed to the ground in front of him. 'What do you see there?'

'Tracks,' said Piglet. 'Paw-marks.' He gave a little squeak of excitement. 'Oh, Pooh! Do you think it's a – a – a Woozle?'

'It may be,' said Pooh. 'Sometimes it is, and sometimes it isn't. You can never tell with paw-marks.'

With these few words he went on tracking, and Piglet, after watching him for a minute or two, ran after him. Winnie-the-Pooh had come to a sudden stop, and was bending over the tracks in a puzzled sort of way.

'What's the matter?' asked Piglet.

'It's a very funny thing,' said Bear, 'but there seem to be *two* animals now. This – whatever-it-was – has been joined by another – whatever-it-is – and the two of them are now proceeding in company. Would you mind coming with me, Piglet, in case they turn out to be Hostile Animals?'

Piglet scratched his ear in a nice sort of way, and said that he had nothing to do until Friday, and would be delighted to come, in case it really *was* a Woozle.

'You mean, in case it really is two Woozles,' said Winnie-the-Pooh, and Piglet said that any-how he had nothing to do until Friday. So off they went together.

There was a small spinney of larch-trees just here, and it seemed as if the two Woozles, if that is what they were, had been going round this

spinney; so round this spinney went Pooh and Piglet after them; Piglet passing the time by telling Pooh what his Grandfather Trespassers W had done to Remove Stiffness after Tracking, and how his Grandfather Trespassers W had suffered in his later years from Shortness of Breath, and other matters of interest, and Pooh wondering what a Grandfather was like, and if perhaps this was Two Grandfathers they were after now, and, if so, whether  he would be allowed to take one home and keep it, and what Christopher Robin would say. And still the tracks went on in front of them. . . .

Suddenly Winnie-the-Pooh stopped, and pointed excitedly in front of him. '*Look!*'

'*What?*' said Piglet, with a jump. And then,

to show that he hadn't been frightened, he jumped up and down once or twice more in an exercising sort of way.

'The tracks!' said Pooh. '*A third animal has joined the other two!*'

'Pooh!' cried Piglet. 'Do you think it is another Woozle?'

'No,' said Pooh, 'because it makes different marks. It is either Two Woozles and one, as it might be, Wizzle, or Two, as it might be, Wizzles and one, if so it is, Woozle. Let us continue to follow them.'

So they went on, feeling just a little anxious now, in case the three animals in front of them were of Hostile Intent. And Piglet wished very much that his Grandfather T. W. were there, instead of elsewhere, and Pooh thought how nice it would be if they met Christopher Robin suddenly but quite accidentally, and only because he liked Christopher Robin so much. And then, all of a sudden, Winnie-the-Pooh stopped again, and licked the tip of his nose in a cooling manner, for he was feeling more hot and anxious than ever in his life before. *There were four animals in front of them!*

'Do you see, Piglet? Look at their tracks! Three, as it were, Woozles, and one, as it was, Wizzle. *Another Woozle has joined them!*'

And so it seemed to be. There were the tracks; crossing over each other here, getting muddled up with each other there; but, quite plainly every now and then, the tracks of four sets of paws.

'I *think*,' said Piglet, when he had licked the tip of his nose too, and found that it brought very little comfort, 'I *think* that I have just remembered something. I have just remembered something that I forgot to do yesterday and shan't be able to do to-morrow. So I suppose I really ought to go back and do it now.'

'We'll do it this afternoon, and I'll come with you,' said Pooh.

'It isn't the sort of thing you can do in the afternoon,' said Piglet quickly. 'It's a very particular morning thing, that has to be done in the morning, and, if possible, between the hours of— What would you say the time was?'

'About twelve,' said Winnie-the-Pooh, looking at the sun.

'Between, as I was saying, the hours of twelve and twelve five. So, really, dear old Pooh, if you'll excuse me— *What's that?*'

Pooh looked up at the sky, and then, as he heard the whistle again, he looked up into the branches of a big oak-tree, and then he saw a friend of his.

'It's Christopher Robin,' he said.

'Ah, then you'll be all right,' said Piglet. 'You'll be quite safe with *him*. Good-bye,' and he trotted off home as quickly as he could, very glad to be Out of All Danger again.

Christopher Robin came slowly down his tree.

'Silly old Bear,' he said, 'what *were* you doing? First you went round the spinney twice by yourself, and then Piglet ran after you and you went round again together, and then you were just going round a fourth time—'

'Wait a moment,' said Winnie-the-Pooh, holding up his paw.

He sat down and thought, in the most thoughtful way he could think. Then he fitted his paw into one of the Tracks . . . and then he scratched his nose twice, and stood up.

'Yes,' said Winnie-the-Pooh.

'I see now,' said Winnie-the-Pooh.

'I have been Foolish and Deluded,' said he, 'and I am a Bear of No Brain at All.'

'You're the Best Bear in All the World,' said Christopher Robin soothingly.

'Am I?' said Pooh hopefully. And then he brightened up suddenly. 'Anyhow,' he said, 'it is nearly Luncheon Time.'

So he went home for it.